Flowers for G

Story by Dawn McMillan

Illustrations by Pat Reynolds

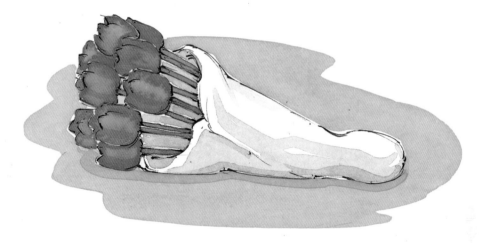

Rigby

A Harcourt Achieve Imprint

www.Rigby.com
1-800-531-5015

Ella came home
and looked for Grandma.

"Mom," said Ella,
"where is Grandma?"

"Grandma is in the hospital," said Mom.

"Oh no!" cried Ella.

"She will come home in two days," said Mom.

"We can go and see her in the hospital."

"I will get some flowers
for Grandma," said Ella.
"She likes the red flowers
in my garden."

6

Ella ran into the garden
to get the flowers.

Mom came to help.

Ella and Mom went to the hospital
to see Grandma.

"The flowers are for Grandma,"
said Ella.

"Hello, Grandma," said Ella.
"Here are some flowers for you."

"Oh thank you, Ella!"
said Grandma.
"I love your red flowers."

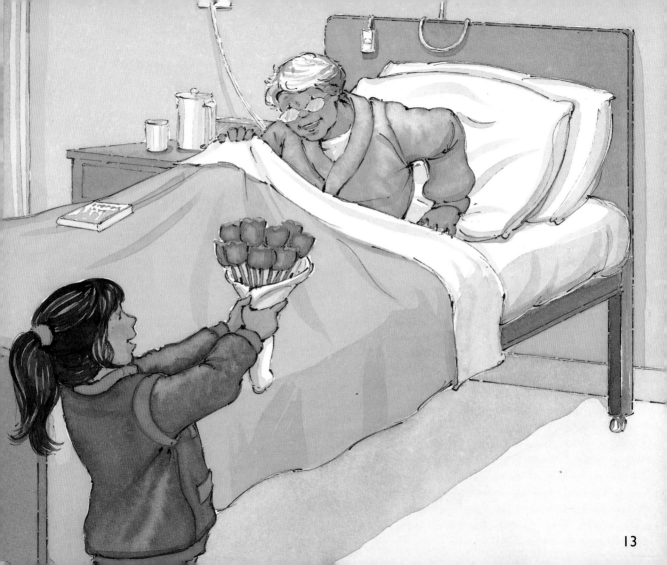

"I am coming home on Friday," said Grandma.
"Your flowers can come home with me."

"I love you, Grandma!"
said Ella.